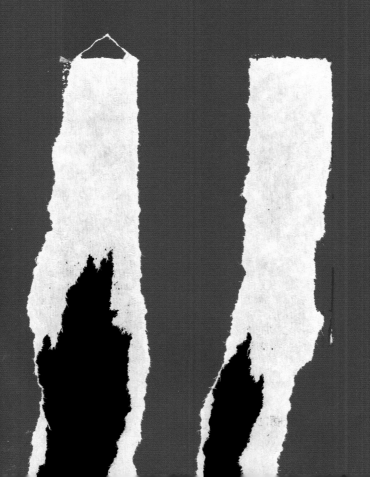

Library of Congress Cataloging-in-Publication Data
Goldilocks and the three bears /illustrated ...by Mireille Levert. p. ... ...ook, New York."
Summary: A little girl walking in the woo... ...nds the house of the ... ...helps herself to
their belongings. ISBN 0-307-10235-1 (alk. p... ...1. Folklore. 2. Bears ... ..., Mireille, ill.
PZ8.G62 2000 398.22—dc21 [E] 99-4366...

Goldilocks
and the Three Bears

illustrated by Mireille Levert

A Golden Book • New York
Golden Books Publishing Company, Inc.,
New York, New York 10106

Once upon a time,
in a cottage in the woods,
there lived three bears.
There was a **great big** papa bear,
a **middle-sized** mama bear,
and a wee little baby **bear**.

Every morning, when the three bears awoke,
they ate porridge out of their special bowls.
Great Big Papa Bear had a great big bowl.
Middle-sized Mama Bear had a middle-sized bowl.
And Wee Little Baby Bear had a teeny-tiny bowl
all his own.

In the afternoon, the three bears took a walk
and afterward read in their special chairs.

Great Big Papa
Bear had a
**great
big** chair.

Middle-sized Mama Bear
had a **middle-sized** chair.

And Wee Little Baby Bear
had a teeny-tiny chair all his own.

In the evening, when the sun went down, the three bears slept in their special beds.

Great Big Papa Bear slept in a **great big** bed.

Middle-sized Mama Bear slept in a **middle-sized** bed.

And Wee Little Baby Bear slept in a teeny-tiny bed all his own.

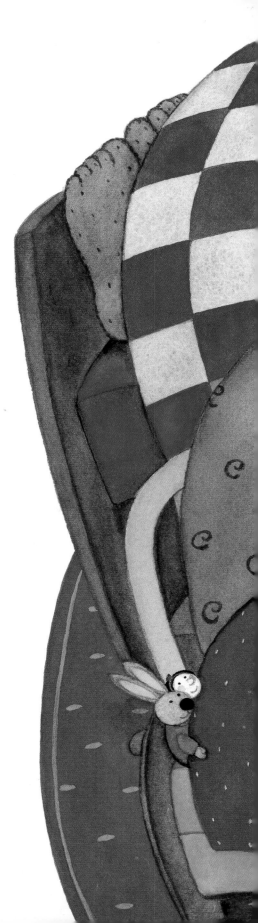

One morning at breakfast, the three
bears sat down to eat their porridge,
but it was way too hot.

"Let's take a walk in the woods," said
Great Big Papa Bear, "until it cools down."
So away they went.

While they were gone,
a little girl named
Goldilocks came by.

She walked up to the window and peeked in.
No one was home.

She saw the three bowls of porridge sitting on
the table. "That porridge looks awfully good," she
thought. "And I'm awfully hungry."

So she tiptoed into the cottage.

First she tasted the porridge
in the **great big** bowl.
"Too hot!" she said.

Then she tasted the porridge
in the **middle-sized** bowl.
"Too cold!" she said.

Finally she tasted the porridge
in the teeny-tiny bowl.
"Mmmmm," said Goldilocks.
The porridge was neither too hot
nor too cold.
It was just right!
Goldilocks gobbled it all up.

Next Goldilocks decided
to sit down for a while.
First she sat in the
great big chair.
"Too hard," she said.

Then she sat in the
middle-sized chair.
"Too soft!" she said.

Finally she sat in the
teeny-tiny chair.
It was neither too hard
nor too soft.
It was just right.
But when she sat down,
the little chair broke!

Goldilocks stood up. She was all right,
but she felt a little sleepy.
She decided to lie down and take a nap.
First she lay on the **great big** bed.
"Too hard!" she said.

Then she lay on the middle-sized bed.
"Too soft!" she said.

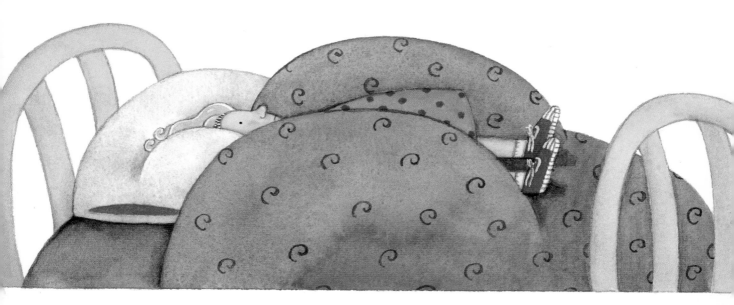

Finally, she lay on the teeny-tiny bed.
It was neither too hard nor too soft.
It was just right.

Goldilocks fell fast asleep.

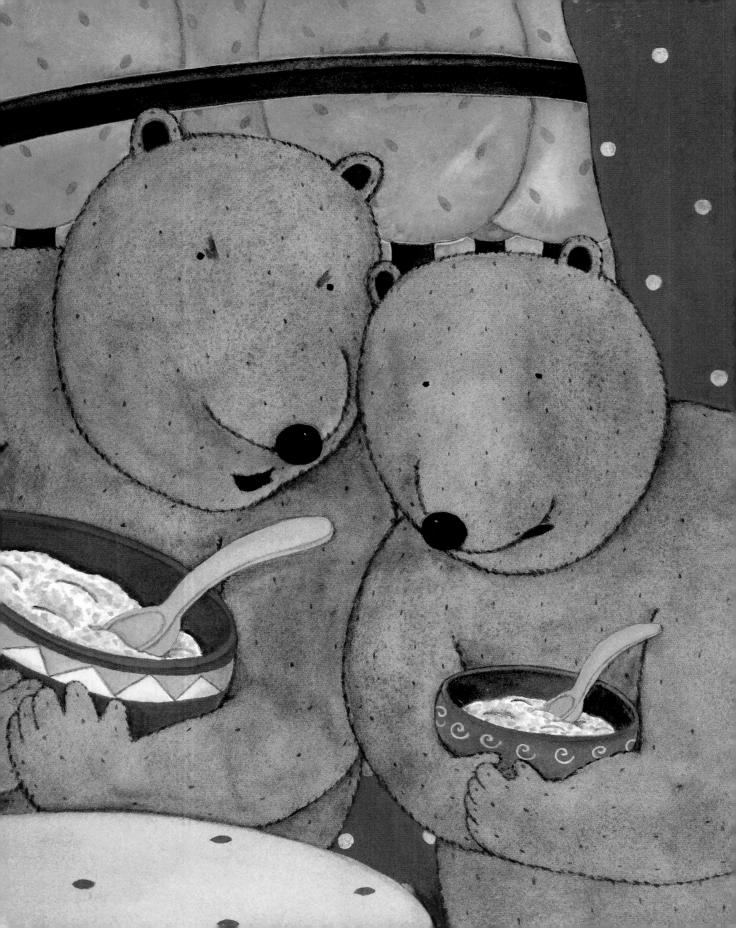

Meanwhile…

The three bears came back from their walk.

They sat down to eat their breakfast.

"Somebody has been eating my porridge!" said Great Big Papa Bear.

"Somebody has been eating my porridge, too!" said Middle-sized Mama Bear.

"Somebody has been eating my porridge and has eaten it all up!" said Wee Little Baby Bear.

The three bears began to look around. **"Somebody has been sitting in my chair!"** said Great Big Papa Bear.

"Somebody has been sitting in my chair, too!" said Middle-sized Mama Bear.

"Somebody has been sitting in my chair, and has broken it all to pieces!" said Wee Little Baby Bear.

The three bears ran and looked at their beds.
"**Somebody has been sleeping in my bed!**" said Great Big Papa Bear.

"**Somebody has been sleeping in my bed, too!**" said Middle-sized Mama Bear.

"Somebody has been sleeping in my bed, and *there she is!*" said Wee Little Baby Bear.

Goldilocks woke up and saw the three bears staring down at her.

"Help!" she cried. She jumped out of bed and headed home as fast as she could.

"**Bye**," said Great Big Papa Bear in his great big voice.

"**Good-bye**," said Middle-sized Mama Bear in her middle-sized voice.

"Bye-bye," said Wee Little Baby Bear in his teeny-tiny voice.

And the three bears never saw Goldilocks again.